Alto and Tango

by Claire Schumacher

WILLIAM MORROW AND COMPANY
New York • 1984

Library of Congress Cataloging in Publication Data
Schumacher, Claire.   Alto and Tango.   Summary: Parting after a summer of singing and
dancing by the sea, two new friends vow to meet when it is summer once again in this part
of the world. [1. Friendship—Fiction. 2. Fishes—Fiction. 3. Birds—Fiction] I. Title.
PZ7.S3914A   1984   [E]   83-13381
ISBN 0-688-02739-3   ISBN 0-688-02740-7 (lib. bdg.)

Alto and Tango

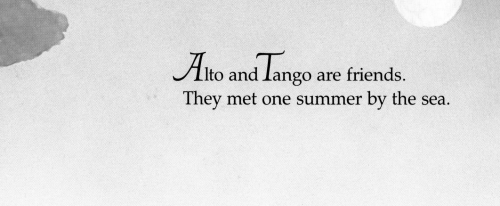

Alto and Tango are friends.
They met one summer by the sea.

Alto likes to sing.

And when Alto sings, Tango dances.

They sang and danced all summer long.
But when the wind blew the leaves from
the trees, they knew they had to part.

Alto said, "I am going to an island very far from here, where the trees don't lose their leaves. The sky is deep blue, and sweet-smelling flowers grow everywhere."

Tango said, "I am going to a warm sea very far from here, where seaweeds grow, and the sand is soft and covered with shells."

They promised to meet when it was summer again in this part of the world. Alto was very sad and raised his wings as high as he could to say good-bye to his friend.

Tango's eyes were red, but since he was in the water, no one could tell he was crying. Tango blew kisses in big bubbles, and the two friends went their separate ways.

Alto almost ran into a big bird.
The bird opened its long sharp beak…

Tango saw a shark swimming toward him,
its jaws stretched wide open...

"Hello," called the big bird as it flew past.
Alto waved back.

The shark was looking for bigger fish
and didn't notice Tango at all.

There was a terrible storm on Alto's way.
I hope the weather is better where you are, Tango,
he thought.

But there was a storm
on Tango's way, too.

Alto had to fly between
the bolts of lightning.

Tango was tossed up and down in the waves. Wherever you may be, Alto, he thought, I hope you're not flying in this weather.

Alto was glad to rest after the storm
and share a ship captain's food.

A ship's cook threw
scraps to Tango.

Alto wanted to rest longer but he still had far to
go. Oh, Tango, he thought, if only I could see you
dancing, my wings wouldn't feel so heavy.

Tango was so tired he could barely swim. Oh,
Alto, he thought, if only I could hear you singing,
it would help me on my way.

That night Alto reached his
island. He slept under the stars
and dreamed about Tango.

Tango reached his
warm sea. He fell asleep
on the soft sand and
dreamed of Alto.

The next morning the sun was hot, and the sky was deep blue. It was summer in that part of the world. Alto felt so good that he began a song for Tango, even though his friend couldn't hear him anymore.

Tango woke up in his warm sea. When he heard an old familiar song, he thought he was still dreaming.

"Tango! Is this your warm sea?"

"Alto! Is this your island?"

And they sang and danced,
happy and together again.